OuTSiDE iN

By Deborah Underwood

Illustrated by Cindy Derby

HOUGHTON MIFFLIN HARCOURT | Boston New York

Once
we were part of Outside
and Outside was part of us.

There was nothing between us.

Now
sometimes even when
we're outside . . .

we're inside.

We forget Outside is there.

So Outside reminds us

with flashes at the window

and slow magic tricks.

It sends the sunset
and shadows inside
to play.

Outside sings to us
with chirps
and rustles
and tap-taps on the roof.

It beckons with smells:
sunbaked,
fresh,
and mysterious.

Outside feeds us.
Sun, rain, and seeds
become warm bread
and berries.

Outside cuddles us
in clothes,
once puffs of cotton.

It holds us
in wooden chairs,
once trees.

We feel Outside
in the warm weight of our cats
and the rough fur of our dogs.

Outside shows us

there is a time to rest

and a time to start fresh.

Outside steals inside:

a spider seeking shelter,

a boxelder bug in the bath,

a tiny snail on kale.

Even rivers come inside:

cool water rushing,

eager to return to the sea.

I'm here,
Outside says.

I miss you.

Outside waits . . .

and we answer.

For Kate —D. U.

For my dear friend Amanda Gaughan—C. D.

hmhbooks.com

Illustrations for this book were made with watercolor and powdered graphite on cold press paper.
Some of the lines were created with dried flower stems and thread soaked in ink.
The text type was set in Expo Sans Pro.
The display type was hand-lettered by Cindy Derby.

Designed by Whitney Leader-Picone

Library of Congress Cataloging-in-Publication Data
Names: Underwood, Deborah, author. | Derby, Cindy, illustrator.
Title: Outside / by Deborah Underwood ; illustrated by Cindy Derby.
Description: Boston ; New York : Houghton Mifflin Harcourt, [2020] |
Summary: Illustrations and easy-to-read text reveal ways nature affects our everyday lives, such as providing food and clothing, and showing when to go to bed and when to get up.
Identifiers: LCCN 2019008355 | ISBN 9781328866820 (hardcover picture book)
Subjects: | CYAC: Nature—Fiction. | Mindfulness (Psychology)—Fiction.
Classification: LCC PZ7.U4193 Out 2020 | DDC [E]—dc23
LC record available at https://lccn.loc.gov/2019008355

Manufactured in Malaysia
TWP 10 9 8 7 6 5 4 3 2 1
4500786546